BBC Children's Books
Published by the Penguin Group
Penguin Books Ltd, 80 Strand, London, WC2R 0RL, England
Penguin Books (USA) Inc., 375 Hudson Street, New York 10014, USA
Penguin Books (Australia) Ltd, 250 Camberwell Road, Camberwell, Victoria
3124, Australia
(A division of Pearson Australia Group PTY Ltd)
Canada, India, New Zealand, South Africa
Published by BBC Children's Books, 2010
Text and design © Children's Character Books
Written by Justin Richards
Images on pages 116,117, 132 and 133 courtesy of NASA
10 9 8 7 6 5 4 3 2 1
ISBN: 9781405907484
Printed in Slovakia

Companion Compendium

TOP TRIVIA FOR TIME TRAVELLERS

Contents

Introduction

The Doctor only accepts the very best people to be his companions. This book provides essential information about the Doctor's companions as well as the Doctor himself. It also tells you some of the things you will need to know if you hope and intend to become one of the Doctor's companions yourself.

Whether the TARDIS takes you to the past, the present, or the future, you will find something in this book that will be relevant and helpful. Learn how to address royalty, send a message in code, and spot which sort of Dalek is trying to exterminate you. There's no substitute for the actual experience of adventuring through space and time, but if anything can help you to stay alive then maybe it's this book. And the Doctor himself, of course.

9

Spotter's Guide to the Doctors

The First Doctor

A crotchety old man who didn't suffer fools gladly. His background was a mystery, and he couldn't control the TARDIS.

The Second Doctor

An eccentric wanderer in space and time. He often seemed out of his depth and confused, but really he knew exactly how to fight the evils of the universe.

The Third Doctor

Distinguished and elegant, exiled to twentieth century Earth by the Time Lords. He defended Earth from alien attack, and constantly tried to win back his freedom.

The Fourth Doctor

Unpredictable but brilliant. Sometimes childishly silly and other times deadly serious. A Jack of all trades, and master of most of them.

The Fifth Doctor

His youthful good looks and open, pleasant face concealed the same depth of experience and intelligence as all the other Doctors.

The Sixth Doctor

Bombastic and theatrical, but deeply caring of his companions and desperate to fight against injustice and oppression.

The Seventh Doctor

An erratic bumbler one moment, but a master planner the next. He sought out his enemies and tidied up unfinished business.

The Eighth Doctor

A charming adventurer. Perhaps the most 'human' of the Doctor's incarnations, he would still stop at nothing to save the world and his friends.

Spotter's Guide to the Doctors

The Ninth Doctor

Last survivor of the Great Time War – or so he thinks. He carried the burden of survival with him and brought an otherworldly perspective to his adventures.

The Tenth Doctor

Revelling in his travels and adventures, this Doctor would not tolerate oppression or injustice. He gave no second chances and his enemies opposed him at their peril.

The Eleventh Doctor

Younger, yet older. He might seem inexperienced, but the youthful looks disguise the same wisdom, determination, ingenuity and passion for justice that the Doctor has always had.

Main Companions
of the
First Doctor

Susan Foreman

The Doctor's granddaughter.

Ian Chesterton and Barbara Wright

School teachers who blundered into the TARDIS.

Dodo Chaplet

London girl looking for a real Police Box.

Vicki

Orphan stranded after a spaceship crash.

Polly Wright and Ben Jackson

Secretary and sailor who met while fighting the War Machines.

Steven Taylor

Space pilot captured by the Mechonoids.

Katarina

Handmaid to the Trojan seer and princess Cassandra.

13

Companions
of the
Second Doctor

Jamie McCrimmon

Highland rebel who met the Doctor in 1746.

Victoria Waterfield

Victorian girl whose father was exterminated by the Daleks.

Zoe Heriot

Brilliant young astrophysicist who worked on a future space station.

Companions
of the
Third Doctor

Brigadier Lethbridge-Stewart

Commander of the British forces in UNIT.

Liz Shaw

UNIT's first scientific advisor.

Jo Grant

The Doctor's scatty assistant at UNIT.

Sarah Jane Smith

Investigative journalist who thought
the Doctor was a 'story'.

Companions
of the
Fourth Doctor

Harry Sullivan

UNIT's medical officer who looked after the regenerated Doctor.

Leela

Warrior of the tribe of Sevateem.

K-9

Robot dog from the future.

The first Romana

Time Lady sent to help the Doctor find the Key to Time.

The second Romana

Regenerated incarnation of Lady Romanadvoratrelundar (her full name!).

Adric

Boy maths genius from an alien planet.

Main Companions
of the
Fifth Doctor

Nyssa

Daughter of a nobleman of Traken who was killed by the Master.

Tegan Jovanka

Air hostess who thought the TARDIS was a real Police Box.

Vislor Turlough

Alien renegade boy exiled to Earth and desperate to escape from school.

Companions
of the
Sixth Doctor

Mel Bush

Computer programmer and keep-fit fanatic.

Peri Brown

American botany student on a longer holiday than she planned.

Companion
of the
Seventh Doctor

Ace

Teenage school girl whisked away in a time storm to work as a waitress in the far future.

19

Companion
of the
Eighth Doctor

Grace Holloway

Surgeon who operated
on the Doctor after
he was shot in San
Francisco.

Companions
of the
Ninth Doctor

Rose Tyler

Shop girl from London who became the Tenth Doctor's best friend. She now lives in an alternate reality.

Captain Jack Harkness

Time Agent from the future, who later became immortal and worked for Torchwood in Cardiff.

Companions
of the
Tenth Doctor

Mickey Smith

Rose Tyler's boyfriend when the Doctor first met her, though he later married Martha Jones.

Donna Noble

Bride-to-be who found herself in the TARDIS when her fiancé betrayed her with the Empress of the Racnoss. She later went travelling with the Doctor.

Martha Jones

Medical student who helped the Doctor against a Plasmavore when the Judoon transported her hospital to the moon.

Companions
of the
Eleventh Doctor

Amy Jessica Pond

Girl who waited years for her 'Raggedy Doctor'
to return and take her away in his TARDIS.

Rory Williams

Amy's fiancé – turned into an
Auton, he waited centuries to be
with Amy again, protecting her
while she slept in the Pandorica.

The Doctor has fought many dangerous enemies over the centuries. Some of them have proved to be more dangerous — and more determined and resilient — than others. This chart shows just how deadly some of the Doctor's more notable enemies can be.

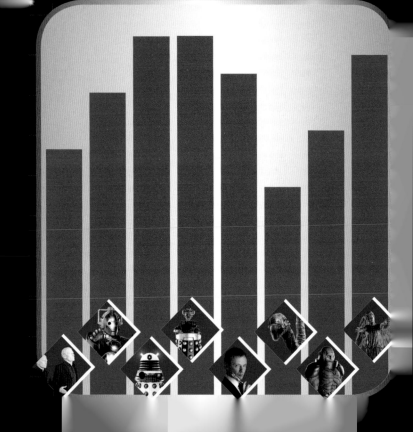

Words of Wisdom

'It's like when you're a kid. The first time they tell you that the world's turning and you just can't quite believe it because everything looks like it's standing still. I can feel it. The turn of the Earth. The ground beneath our feet is spinning at a thousand miles an hour and the entire planet is hurtling around the sun at 67,000 miles an hour, and I can feel it. We're falling through space, you and me, clinging to the skin of this tiny little world, and if we let go... That's who I am.'
The Ninth Doctor

'Didn't anyone ever tell you, there's one thing you never put in a trap? If you're smart. If you value your continued existence, if you have any plans about seeing tomorrow – there is one thing you never, ever put in a trap... Me.'
The Eleventh Doctor

'He's like fire and ice and rage. He's like the night and the storm in the heart of the sun. He's ancient and forever. He burns at the centre of time and he can see the turn of the universe.'
Tim Latimer

'I'm the Doctor. I'm a Time Lord. I'm from the planet Gallifrey in the constellation of Kasterborous. I'm 903 years old and I'm the man who's going to save your lives and all six billion of the people on the planet below. You got a problem with that?'
The Tenth Doctor

'Hello, I'm the Doctor. Basically – run!'
The Eleventh Doctor

Recurring Nightmares

Some of the monsters the Doctor has fought have returned time and again to do battle with him. Which monsters are you most likely to meet if you travel in the TARDIS? Of course, you can never be certain, but the chart shows which monsters the Doctor has encountered most often. So it might give you some clues.

How to Tie a Bow Tie

Knowing how to tie a bow tie is a skill that is useful across the universe. It's actually very similar to tying a shoelace. Study the diagrams below and practice in front of a mirror. You never know when you might need to infiltrate the launch party for a new — and dangerous — scientific invention, or get to the President's cocktail party ahead of the Cybermen.

1 Put the bow tie around your neck and under your collar. Hang it so that the end on your right is a couple of inches longer than the end on your left.

2 Cross the longer end over the shorter end. Keep it quite close to your neck, so that when it is completely tied, it isn't dangling down.

3 Pass the longer end up through the loop, to make a loose knot.

4

Hold the loose end that is now on your right and fold the end back to form a loop. Pinch it between your thumb and index finger. Try to double the right side of the tie (which starts on the left side of your neck) over itself to make the loop. Hold this loop, which will be the front loop of the bow tie, between your shirt's collar points.

5

Move the left side of the tie (the one which you passed up through the loop in step 3) over the front of the bow.

6

Make a new loop with the left side, just as you did with the first one. While still holding the loop you just made, double the end over itself.

7

Position the new loop behind the front loop but facing the opposite way. Pinch the loops together with your thumb and push the second loop into the knot behind the front loop. Push the end of this loop into the hole behind the front loop. On one side, the loop will be at the front. On the other, it will be at the back.

8

Tighten the knot by pulling the two loops together. To untie the bow, pull on the tails. Good luck, it's pretty tricky!

The
Time Lords

The Time Lords are gone, destroyed in the Great Time War never to return...

But it is just possible that apart from the Doctor, another Time Lord – or Time Lady – might have survived. Over the years, and down the centuries, the Doctor has encountered many of his own race outside Gallifrey. Listed here are some of the Time Lords to look out for.

The Doctor

An eternal wanderer in time and space. Generally thought to be the last of the Time Lords. He travels in a Type 40 TARDIS and fights injustice and oppression wherever he finds it.

The Master

A renegade Time Lord and former friend of the Doctor, now one of his bitterest enemies. The Doctor and the Master have encountered each other in many different incarnations.

POLICE PUBLIC BOX

Omega

The stellar engineer who created a black hole to give the Time Lords the power they needed to travel in time. He was lost in the resulting supernova and presumed dead.

Borusa

One of the Doctor's tutors at the Academy, Borusa eventually became president of the Time Lords. But he abused his power and tried to become President Eternal.

Other Time Lords

Away from Gallifrey, the Doctor has also met the so-called Meddling Monk who tried to change history to his own advantage, misguided chemistry expert the Rani, and Drax, an engineer and school friend of the Doctor's. He also encountered the surviving brain of Morbius – a former Time Lord President who wanted to conquer other worlds but was executed for his crimes.

Rassilon

Arguably the greatest President of the Time Lords, who came to them in their hour of need to fight the Great Time War against the Daleks. He was corrupted by war and power and sought to save Gallifrey at any cost.

Words of Wisdom

'I tell you, before your ancestors had turned the first wheel, the people of my world had reduced movement through the farthest reaches of space to a game for children.'
The First Doctor

'Our lives are different from anybody else's. That's the exciting thing. Nobody in the universe can do what we're doing.'
The Second Doctor

'A straight line may be the shortest distance between two points, but it is by no means the most interesting.'
The Third Doctor

'I walk in Eternity.' **The Fourth Doctor**

'There's always something to look at, if you open your eyes.'
The Fifth Doctor

'If I stopped to question the wisdom of my actions I'd never have left Gallifrey.'
The Sixth Doctor

POLICE PUBLIC CALL BOX

POLICE TELEPHONE
FREE
FOR USE OF
PUBLIC
ADVICE & ASSISTANCE
OBTAINABLE IMMEDIATELY
OFFICERS & CARS
RESPOND TO ALL CALLS
PULL TO OPEN

'Funny old business, time; it delights in frustrating your plans.'
The Seventh Doctor

'What a sentimental old thing this TARDIS is.'
The Eighth Doctor

'TARDIS – it stands for Time And Relative Dimension In Space.'
The Ninth Doctor

'It used to be easy. When the Time Lords kept their eye on everything, you could hop between realities, home in time for tea. Then they died, took it all with them. The walls of reality closed, the worlds were sealed. Everything became that bit less kind.'
The Tenth Doctor

'Amy Pond, there's something you better understand about me, 'cause it's important and one day your life may depend on it. I am definitely a madman with a box.'
The Eleventh Doctor

Plenty of Rooms
Inside

The TARDIS, as everyone knows, is bigger inside than outside. But not many people realise how much bigger it really is. There's more than just the vast control room — it's like an entire world or city inside. Here are just some of the rooms you might find on a quick tour.

Swimming Pool

A good place to relax or get some exercise.

Library

Last time the Doctor checked, the TARDIS Library was inside the swimming pool. But it's probably sorted itself out since.

Art Gallery

Contains a fine collection of paintings, sculptures and holograms.

Power Room

Just one of the many maintenance and technical areas inside the timeship.

Living Areas

There are many bedrooms, bathrooms and recreational areas.

Wardrobe

Contains clothing and accessories from just about every time period on every inhabited world. And a few other places too.

The Cloister Room

An area for meditation and solitude. But beware – if the Cloister Bell rings, it means the TARDIS is in terrible danger.

The War of the Worlds by H G Wells

The Time Machine by H G Wells

Hamlet (First Folio) by William Shakespeare
(as dictated to the Doctor)

Love's Labours Won by William Shakespeare

THE BODY IN THE LIBRARY BY AGATHA CHRISTIE

Harry Potter and the Philospher's Stone
by J K Rowling

The Signalman and Other Stories
by Charles Dickens

DEATH IN THE CLOUDS BY AGATHA CHRISTIE

The **TARDIS Library**

The TARDIS boasts one of the largest libraries in all creation. Finding the book you're after can be difficult, but at least you won't have to worry about getting a fine for an overdue book — the TARDIS can make sure it's returned *before* you even borrowed it.

A Journal of Impossible Things by Verity Newman

Origins of the Universe by Oolon Colluphid

Teach Yourself Tibetan

TARDIS MANUAL (TYPE 40 VARIANT)

The Dalek Survival Guide

MOUNTAINEERING FOR BEGINNERS

Famous
Last Words

'Grandfather – I belong with you.'
Susan to the Doctor as he leaves her on Earth

'I'll see you again, Mister.'
Martha to the Doctor after defeating the Master

'I love you.'
Rose to the Doctor's image at Bad Wolf Bay

'The process is simple.'
K-9 explains to the Doctor

'You know, you act like such a lonely man. But look at you – you've got the biggest family on Earth.'
Sarah Jane Smith to the Doctor

'See you, Boss.'
Mickey Smith to the Doctor

'Please, don't make me go back...'
Donna before she loses her memory

'Now I'll never know if I was right.'
Adric, about to die in a space freighter crash

'I won't forget you, you know.'
Jamie McCrimmon to the Doctor

...with her mum
...owell Estate in
...uth London.

Spends Time
Shop Assistant at Henrik's department store.

Relatives
Mum (Jackie). Father Peter Tyler killed in car accident in 1987.

First met the Doctor
At Henrik's store. The Doctor saved Rose from attacking Autons.

Left the Doctor

Stayed on a parallel Earth with her mother and a 'parallel' version of her father. But returned to help the Doctor on several subsequent occasions.

Enemies Faced

Daleks, Cybermen, Autons, Cassandra, Gelth, Slitheen, Jagrafess, Reapers, Empty Child, Sycorax, Werewolf, Krillitanes, Clockwork Androids, the Wire, the Beast, the Abzorbaloff, Isolus Child, Davros...

Friends and Allies

Mickey Smith, Captain Jack Harkness, Adam Mitchell, Harriet Jones, Charles Dickens, Sarah Jane Smith, K-9...

Friendly Robots

The Doctor has met many robots and races of robots in his travels. Some have been dastardly killing machines created to wage war. Some robots have been reprogrammed to become hostile — like Robot K-1 met by the Fourth Doctor, or the so-called Robots of Death reprogrammed by madman Taren Capel, or the Heavenly Host that served Max Capricorn on board the starship *Titanic*...

But most robots are servile and harmless, obeying their orders without question or emotion.

A few, a very few, have helped the Doctor and some he has even counted as friends.

K-9

Robot dog created by professor Marius and given to the Doctor after he helped defeat an alien virus swarm. There have been several versions of K-9. One stayed on Gallifrey with the Doctor's friend Leela. Another travelled into another universe with Time Lady Romana, and a third — later rebuilt — the Doctor gave to his good friend Sarah Jane Smith.

Anne Droid

A deadly gameshow hostess robot which was reprogrammed to attack the Daleks – and paid the ultimate price for it.

Kamelion

A shape-changing android which the Doctor rescued from the Master, but which he was later forced to destroy.

Gadget

A utility robot that proved invaluable to the Doctor in saving the crew of Bowie Base One on Mars from The Flood.

Words of Wisdom – Gallifrey

'The sky's a burnt orange, with the Citadel enclosed in a mighty glass dome, shining under the twin suns. Beyond that, the mountains go on forever – slopes of deep red grass, capped with snow.'

The Tenth Doctor

'There was a war – a time war. The last Great Time War. My race fought a race called the Daleks. For the sake of all creation. And they lost. They lost. Everyone lost. They're all gone now. My family. My friends. Even that sky. Oh, you should have seen it, that old planet. The second sun would rise in the south and the mountain would shine. The leaves on the trees were silver and they'd light the sky every morning like it was on fire.' – The Tenth Doctor

'They used to call it the Shining World of the Seven Systems. And on the Continent of Wild Endeavour, in the Mountains of Solace and Solitude, there stood the Citadel of the Time Lords. The oldest and most mighty race in the universe... looking down on the galaxies below... sworn never to interfere, only to watch. Children of Gaillfrey, taken from their families at the age of eight, to enter the Academy. Some say that's where it all began—when he was a child. That's when the Master saw eternity. As a novice he was taken for initiation. He stood in front of the Untempered Schism. It's a gap in the fabric of reality, through which can be seen the whole of reality. You stand there, eight years old, staring at the raw power of time and space, just a child. Some would be inspired, some would run away, and some would go mad.' – The Tenth Doctor

TV Channels
of the Universe

Between adventures, when life becomes slightly more boring, there's nothing better than catching up on the latest soap opera or checking the news. Here are some TV and Holo-Channels that are worth looking out for.

AMNN	New York-based international news channel, fronted by Trinity Wells.
BBC 1	Blue Peter – Learn how to make a Slitheen Spaceship Cake and walk like a Cyberman.
	Topical interviews with Sharon Osborne, Ann Widdecombe, Derek Acorah, and McFly.
	If you're in 1953, check out the Coronation.
	2012 for the London Olympics.
BBC3	*The Passing Parade* - gives live coverage of the archaeological dig at Devil's End (opposite the rugby on BBC 1).
	Various other Confidential programmes throughout the evening.
BBC News	Covers major news stories like a Slitheen ship crashing into Big Ben, and the invasion of Earth by Cybermen. If planets suddenly appear in the sky, then *BBC News* is there.
	Election coverage – with Harold Saxon riding high in the latest opinion polls.
Bad Wolf	Latest on the Face of Boe's child.
Channel 44,000	Beaming the latest gameshows directly into viewers' eyeballs.
	Big Brother – with disintegration evictions.
	The Weakest Link – hosted by the Anne Droid.
	What not to Wear – with robot hostesses TRIN-E and ZU-ZANA.
	Call My Bluff – with real guns.
	Ground Force – losing contestants are turned into compost.
	Stars in their Eyes – Sing or be blinded.
	Wipeout.

Spaceship Crashes

Travelling in space can be hazardous – beware!
You might crash into a famous landmark, or into
a star or a black hole. Even travelling through
hyperspace, you have to watch out that your
ship doesn't hit another hyperspace vehicle, or
even materialise in the same space as another
ship – that can be nasty.

Listed here are just some examples of spacesh
disasters you would do well to avoid.

Space Pig Crash

A Slitheen spaceship piloted
by an augmented pig
clipped the clock tower of
the Palace of Westminster
before splashing down in
the River Thames. Turns out
it was all perfectly planned
to get publicity and distract
attention from the real
Slitheen takeover.

The Wreck of the Byzantium

The spaceship Byzantium,
carrying what was thought
to be the last of the
Weeping Angels, crashed
into an Aplan Temple.
Luckily, the building had
been unoccupied for
centuries. Unluckily, it
was hit by surviving
Weeping Angels.

Black Holes

...ships have been lost ... escape from the *Hyperion* ... the ... of Tartarus. Most ... ous of all black holes ... K37 GEM 5 – a black hole ... monitored from the relative safety of Sanctuary Base 6, crewed by humans and Ood, which was set up on an impossible planet that actually orbited the black hole.

Starship Titanic

Sabotaged by its owner, Max Capricorn, the *Titanic* almost crashed into Earth – narrowly missing Buckingham Palace as the Doctor managed to steer it to safety. Almost all the crew and passengers perished in the initial meteoroid strike engineered by Max Capricorn.

...on ...droids

...forms are a perpetual ... to space travellers. ... Ponder the fate of the *Mme de Pompadour*, which was lost with all hands – despite being equipped with the latest clockwork-powered repair androids.

Stellar Disruption

Ordinary stars are usual... charted and can easil... avoided. But bewar... s... that are abou... s...nova. Or sta... ...ord... SS Pe... ...iji...

There are many reasons why the Doctor's friends and companions leave the TARDIS. Some choose to move on, for others, sadly, the decision is taken out of their hands.

In the list below, Peri appears twice as there is some temporal confusion as to whether she was shot by the Warlord Yrcanos after having her brain replaced by a giant slug, or married him. Captain Jack was exterminated by the Daleks, but revived by Rose when infected with the power of the Time Vortex.

Left To Get Married
Susan Foreman
Vicki
Jo Grant
Leela
Peri Brown

Left by Choice

Ian Chesterton
Barbara Wright
Steven Taylor
Dodo Chaplet
Ben Jackson
Polly Wright
Victoria Waterfield
Liz Shaw
Harry Sullivan
K-9

Romana
Nyssa
Tegan Jovanka
Vislor Turlough
Mel Bush
Grace Holloway
Captain Jack Harkness
Mickey Smith
Martha Jones

Died Helping the Doctor
Adric
Katarina
Peri Brown
Captain Jack Harkness

Unknown
Ace
Amy Pond
Rory Williams

Left Unwillingly
Jamie McCrimmon
Zoe Heriot
Sarah Jane Smith
Rose Tyler
Donna Noble

Left by Choice
Left to get Married
Died Helping the Doctor
Left Unwillingly
Unknown

Alien Weaknesses

When faced with a hostile alien
creature, it is useful to know
where their weak points lie.

Weeping Angel

Only weakness is the
inability to move while
being observed – so
don't blink!

Dalek

No real weaknesses,
but the eyestalk is
generally considered
a vulnerable point to
attack. Bastic bullets
are best.

Sontaran

A blow to the probic
vent, at the back of the
neck, can disable a
Sontaran.

Cyberman

Unable to cope with direct input of emotions. Solvents can dissolve their plastic components.

Slitheen (and other Raxicoricofallapatorians)

Acids – even weak acids like vinegar – can dissolve and destroy the calcium-based creatures.

Autons

The only way to destroy an Auton is to defeat the Nestene Consciousness that controls it.

Krillitanes

Allergic to their own secreted oil, which burns them. In extreme cases, they explode.

Making History

The Doctor has met many famous people from Earth history — and claims to have met many more. Just some of them are listed on this timeline.

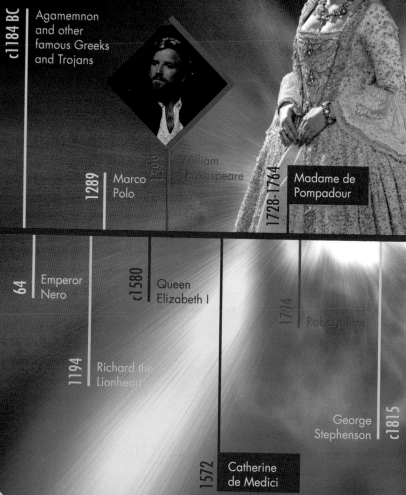

c1184 BC — Agamemnon and other famous Greeks and Trojans

1289 — Marco Polo

1500 — William Shakespeare

1728–1764 — Madame de Pompadour

64 — Emperor Nero

c1580 — Queen Elizabeth I

1794 — Robespierre

1194 — Richard the Lionheart

c1815 — George Stephenson

1572 — Catherine de Medici

1881 Wyatt Earp, Doc Holliday, Johnny Ringo

1940 Winston Churchill

1879 Queen Victoria

1869 Charles Dickens

c1888 Van Gogh

Watch Out!

Travelling in the TARDIS often means travelling into danger. Spotting trouble is a key skill for a time-space adventurer. Here are some clues that things might be about to go horribly wrong.

Mauve for Danger

The universally-recognised colour to signify danger is mauve. Except on Earth, where it's red.

Shadows

Pay close attention to shadows – they can give you all sorts of clues as to what's about to come round the corner. But if you seem to have more shadows than you should, then it might be too late – beware the Vashta Nerada.

If the Doctor says this to you, then be worried.
Be very worried.

Unexpected Movement

If something seems to have moved when it shouldn't have,
that might be a problem. Pay especially close attention to:

* Shop window dummies

* Wheelie bins

* Weeping Angel statues

No One at Home

Deserted spaceships, houses, laboratories, military bases...
You have to ask yourself – where did everyone go?

Too Good to be True

If something seems too good to be true, then it probably is –
whether it's a rare mineral gift from aliens, suddenly finding some
advanced technology, election commitments by Harold Saxon, or
the promise to take you and your mates to an alien planet if you'll
just help the Sontarans invade Earth.

Reflections

You might catch a glimpse of an invisible, mythical
creature in a mirror or a puddle of water. Or you might
be able to use its reflection to fight an otherwise
invisible enemy. Also, beware beautiful but strange
young ladies who don't show up in mirrors.

Martha Jones

Home

Martha lives in London.

Relatives

Mum (Francine), Dad (Clive), sister (Tish), Brother (Leo). She marries Mickey Smith. Her cousin Adeola Oshodi was killed by the Cybermen at Torchwood Tower.

First met the Doctor

In the street on the way to work at Royal Hope Hospital. However, he had travelled back in time to make a point and first met Martha at the hospital, which was then transported to the moon by the Judoon.

Left the Doctor

Left after defeating the Master and resetting Earth's timeline. She later called in the Doctor to help battle the Sontarans, and helped in the fight against Davros and the Daleks.

Enemies Faced

Plasmavore, Carrionites, Macra, Daleks, Lazarus Creature, Sentient star, the Family of Blood, the Master, Sontarans, Davros...

Friends and Allies

William Shakespeare, Lazlo, Joan Redfern, Captain Jack Harkness, Jenny – the Doctor's daughter, Donna Noble...

Alien Battle Cries
and Sayings

Daleks

Exterminate!

Cybermen

Delete – delete – delete.

Sontarans

Sontar-ha!

The Empty Child

Are you my Mummy?

The Master

I am the Master, and you will obey me.

Judoon

Category - Human.

59

Morse Code

...rse code is used to transmit information using a rhythm of short and long pulses – dots and dashes. It was invented in the 1840s for use in early telegraph communications, and later adapted for wireless radio. It can also be handy if you need to send a message using sound or light. The Doctor once signalled to UNIT to help against the Autons by flashing the brake lights of a coach in which he was held captive by the Master.

...most common form of distress signal in Morse Code is SOS – three ...followed by three dashes, then three more dots. In fact, this signal is ...istinctive pattern that just happens to be the same as the letters SOS. ...ter it was devised, people tried to work out what SOS stood for – the ...most common suggestion being Save Our Souls. Nowadays, a distress signal is more likely to be spoken and takes the form: 'Mayday', ...hich is actually the French 'M'aider' meaning 'help me'.

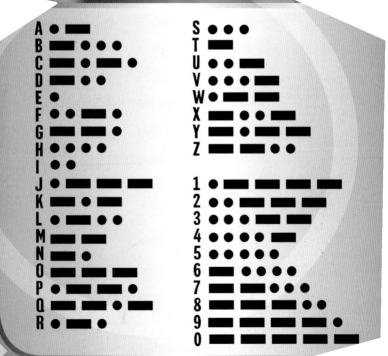

Words of Wisdom

'Homo sapiens – what an inventive, invincible species. It's only a few million years since they crawled up out of the mud and learned to walk. Puny, defenceless bipeds. They've survived flood, famine and plague. They've survived cosmic wars and holocausts. And now, here they are out among the stars, waiting to begin a new life. Ready to outsit eternity. They're indomitable… indomitable.'

The Fourth Doctor

'I love humans. Always seeing patterns in things that aren't there.'

The Eighth Doctor

'Look at these people, these human beings. Consider their potential. From the day they arrive on this planet and blinking, step into the sun, there is more to see than can ever be seen, more to do… No, hold on, sorry that's *The Lion King*. But the point still stands.'

The Tenth Doctor

'When you go back to the stars and tell others of this planet, when you tell them of its riches, its people, its potential, when you talk of the Earth, then make sure that you tell them this: It is defended.'

The Tenth Doctor

'There's no such thing as an ordinary human.'

The Tenth Doctor

Little and Large

The Doctor has met all manner of creatures on his travels – of all shapes and sizes. Some are microscopically small, like the Virus Swarm that infected medics and patients at the Bi-Al Foundation in the year 5,000. Others are as enormous as the planet Magla which is actually a giant amoeba that has grown a crusty shell. Some are as insubstantial as a shadow from the Howling Halls or the dreaded Vashta Nerada – piranhas of the air. Some – like the Daemons – can change their size. Many others are about the same size as a human being...

Isolus Child

Adipose Child

K-9

Zocci

Moxx of Balhoon

Sontaran

Hath

Human

Weeping Angel

Earth Reptiles

Judoon

Cyberman

Dalek

Slitheen

Vespiform

Nestene Consciousness

The Beast

Pyrovile

Macra

Jagrafess

Star Whale

Sentient Sun in the Toraji System

Planets of the Solar System

The solar system consists of all those objects that are caught in our sun's gravity. There are traditionally said to be nine planets in our solar system – all orbiting our sun. But Pluto, the smallest of these is now classed as a 'dwarf planet' as it is so small.

Jupiter

The largest planet – 2½ times the mass of all the other planets put together. One of its moons – Ganymede – is larger than the planet Mercury. Jupiter is named after the Roman leader of the gods (also called Jove).

Mercury

Closest to the sun, and the smallest 'real' planet. Named after the messenger of the gods in Roman mythology.

Earth

Home to the human race. An attractive, habitable planet that has been the object of many alien attacks and attempted invasions.

Venus

About the same size as Earth, but much drier with a denser atmosphere, mainly of carbon dioxide. Named after the Roman goddess of love and beauty (and the only planet named after a female figure).

Mars

The so-called 'red planet' gets its colour from rust (iron oxide) in the soil. Traditional home of the Ice Warriors, and the enigmatic Flood. Named after the Roman god of war.

Pluto

Discovered in 1930 and named after the Roman god of the underworld, Pluto is no longer classified as a planet, but as a dwarf planet. The other dwarf planets are: Ceres, Haumea, Makemake, and Eris.

Saturn

Famous for its rings, which are small particles orbiting the planet. Professor Marius, who invented K-9, worked on a hospital asteroid close to Saturn. Named after the Roman god of farming and harvest.

Neptune

The outermost planet, if you discount Pluto, with a very active weather system. Named after the Roman god of the sea.

Uranus

The only planet to orbit the sun on its side, so it spins 'over and over' rather than 'sideways' like the other planets. Named after the Roman embodiment of the sky.

65

Citizens of the Universe

The Doctor's companions have come from all walks of life,
and all kinds of backgrounds, cultures, and planets.

Human from Past
Katarina
Jamie McCrimmon
Victoria Waterfield

Human from Future
Vicki
Steven Taylor
Zoe Heriot
Leela

Robot
K-9
Kamelion

Other Alien
Adric
Nyssa
Vislor Turlough

Human from Present Day
Barbara Wright
Ian Chesterton
Dodo Chaplet
Ben Jackson
Polly Wright
Liz Shaw
Jo Grant
Sarah Jane Smith
Harry Sullivan
Tegan Jovanka

Peri Brown
Mel Bush
Grace Holloway
Ace
Rose Tyler
Mickey Smith
Martha Jones
Donna Noble
Amy Pond
Rory Williams

Alien - Time Lord
Susan Foreman
Romana

Human from Past
Human from Present Day
Human from Future
Time Lord
Other Alien
Robot

Sarah Jane Smith

Home

Originally from
South Croydon,
Sarah Jane now lives
on Bannerman Road.

Spends Time

Investigative journalist. She
has written for many papers
and magazines, including the
prestigious *Metropolitan*.

Relatives

Aunt Lavinia Smith was a famous
virologist – the Doctor even
read her paper on the teleological
response of the virus.
Aunt Lavinia had a ward called
Brendan. Sarah Jane now has an
adopted son, Luke.

Left the Doctor

Left the Doctor when he was summoned back to Gallifrey for a Presidential Resignation ceremony. She has met him several times since and they have remained the best of friends.

Enemies faced

Sontarans, dinosaurs, Daleks, Exxilons, Ice Warriors, Giant Spiders, Robot K-1, Wirrn, Davros, Cybermen, Zygons, Anti-Man, Sutekh and his robot Mummies, Androids, Kraals, Morbius, Krynoid, Mandragora Energy, Eldrad, Krillitanes, and many others with her son Luke and his friends.

Friends and Allies

K-9, Brigadier Lethbridge-Stewart, Sergeant Benton, Captain Mike Yates (rtd), Harry Sullivan, Luke's friends Clyde, Rani, Maria. Mr Smith – an alien computer.

First met the Doctor

Sarah Jane went into the TARDIS, believing the Doctor was responsible for kidnapping noted scientists. The Doctor was also trying to discover what had happened to the scientists – who had been taken by Commander Linx, a Sontaran stranded in medieval England.

Doctor!!

You might need the Doctor's help on any planet, or even in any country on Earth. Normally, the TARDIS will translate your words into the local language, just as you can understand what the local people say. But if you need to ask for the Doctor and the TARDIS isn't there or has suffered a major breakdown, do you know how to do it? Here's how to call: 'Doctor!' in various useful languages.

Doctor!
[English]

Doctor!
[Spanish]

Dottore!
[Italian]

Doutor!
[Portuguese]

Docteur!
[French]

Tohtori!
[Finnish]

Doktor!
[German]

Ka Faraq Gatri!
[Dalek]

Medicus!
[Latin]

Доктор!
[Russian]

Karshtakavaar!
[Draconian]

71

How to
Spot the Master

The Master is an expert at disguising himself. Don't let him fool you. Be prepared to spot the Master whatever form he takes or disguise he adopts.

Incarnations of the Master:

Bearded and Mephisophelean – nemesis of the Third Doctor

Emaciated near-cadaver – fought the Fourth Doctor

A new (stolen) body at last – archenemy of the Fifth, Sixth and Seventh Doctors

Harold Saxon –
alias The Master

Disguises:

Telecomms engineer

Military Officer

Adjudicator from the future

Police Commissioner from Sirius 4

Mystic

Sir Gilles Estram

Respected politician

Professor Yana

Presidential hopeful

Portreeve of Castrovalva

Hoodie

Words of Wisdom

'There are worlds out there where the sky is burning, and the sea's asleep, and the rivers dream. People made of smoke, and cities made of song. Somewhere there's danger, somewhere there's injustice. And somewhere else, the tea's getting cold...'

Seventh Doctor

'Think you've seen it all? Think again. Outside those doors, we might see anything. We could find new worlds, terrifying monsters, impossible things. And if you come with me, nothing will ever be the same again.'

Tenth Doctor

'Do you wanna come with me? Because if you do, then I should warn you – you're gonna see all sorts of things: ghosts from the past, aliens from the future, the day the Earth died in a ball of flame. It won't be quiet, it won't be safe, and it won't be calm. But I'll tell you what it will be – the trip of a lifetime.'

Ninth Doctor

Phonetic Alphabet

The Phonetic Alphabet is used by organisations throughout the world to identify letters unambiguously so there is no mistake about letters which might otherwise sound the same. It was developed originally in the 1920s and different countries and organisations had their own versions. It has evolved into the standard form used today by organisations like the police, NATO military forces, and UNIT.

Letter	Code Word	Letter	Code Word
A	Alfa	N	November
B	Bravo	O	Oscar
C	Charlie	P	Papa
D	Delta	Q	Quebec
E	Echo	R	Romeo
F	Foxtrot	S	Sierra
G	Golf	T	Tango
H	Hotel	U	Uniform
I	India	V	Victor
J	Juliet	W	Whiskey
K	Kilo	X	X-ray
L	Lima	Y	Yankee
M	Mike	Z	Zulu

Where Have We Landed?

Can you feel the floor vibrating slightly

YES

NO

You are likely to be inside a vehicle

You are probably stationary - in a building or vehicle that isn't moving

Find a window or door and look outside

Are you on a planet or in space?

PLANET

SPACE

Are you stationary? (see above)

NO

YES

NO

You are in a spaceship

Is the place deserted or showing signs of damage?

You are probably on a spacestation

YES

You are probably on a drifting spaceship

START

TARDIS LANDS

STEP OUTSIDE

Can you see the sky?

NO

YES

CAN'T TELL – IT'S CLOUDY OR RAINING

How many suns are there?

MORE THAN ONE

ONE

You are not on Earth. This is an alien planet.

Does this look like Earth - blue sky, green grass, recognisable trees, plants, humans, buildings, cars...?

Probably Britain

FISSION REACTOR OUTPUT

What can you smell?

PETROL

COAL AND CHARCOAL BURNING

You could be in the present day

You may well be in the past

You are probably in the future

BE CAREFUL!!

Other Worlds in Other Skies

You might think you've arrived on Earth, but can you be sure? The Doctor has found himself on a world that looks like Earth several times, only to discover he isn't where he thought he was at all. When you step out of the TARDIS, you might be on another world or in a parallel reality, even though you're pretty sure it's the picturesque seaside resort of Cromer in Norfolk. Even the Doctor's most dedicated companions have been caught out like that.

A Steel Sky

Even if you seem to be in a jungle, you might actually be on a spacestation, or a space ship like the Ark, carrying the vegetation and animals from doomed planet Earth to a new home.

Android Training Village

If the people are behaving oddly, the calendars have the same date for every day, and the ivy is made of plastic then you could be in a sophisticated android training village created by the monstrous Kraals, who are planning to infiltrate Earth with robot doubles of people.

Pete's World

Lots of Zeppelins over the modern London skyline is a bit of a clue that things have gone wrong. You might be on the parallel world where Rose's dad, Pete Tyler, is still alive – and the Cybermen are about to take over.

Wrong Turning

Every decision you take can change not just your own life, but the whole of history. Don't let one of the Pantheon of Discord talk you into taking a wrong turning, or things could turn out very badly for everyone. If you see BAD WOLF written everywhere, it may already be too late.

The Dream Lord

Dreaming or waking – which is which? If a speck of psychic pollen from the candle meadows of Karrass don Slava gets up your nose or into the TARDIS systems you might have trouble working it out. Look for any telltale clue – and choose your reality wisely.

K-9

Home

Originally from the Bi-Al Foundation, K-9 now lives with Sarah Jane on Bannerman Road. (Previous K-9 models have settled on Gallifrey and in the Exo-space Time Continuum.)

Spends Time

Protecting Mistress Sarah Jane and helping the Doctor. Master.

Relatives

K-9 Mark 1, K-9 Mark 2, and the original K-9 Mark 3 before he needed rebuilding by the Doctor after battling the Krillitanes.

First met the Doctor

At the Bi-Al Foundation, a hospital asteroid in the year 5,000 where K-9 was built by Professor Marius.

Left the Doctor

K-9 Mark 1 left the Doctor to stay with Leela on Gallifrey. K-9 Mark 2 went with Romana into E-Space. The Doctor left K-9 Mark 3 as a present for Sarah Jane Smith, and they met properly when Sarah Jane helped the Doctor against the Krillitanes.

Enemies faced

Alien Virus Swarm, Usurians, the Oracle, Vardans, Sontarans, Graff Vynda-K, Pirate Captain and his Polyphase Avatron (robot parrot), Ogri, Count Grendel, the Shadow, Lady Adrasta, Mandrels, Nimon, Meglos, Marshmen, Vampire Lords, Rorvik and his slavers, Krillitanes, Daleks, and many others with Sarah, her son Luke, and his friends.

Friends and Allies

Leela, Romana, Adric, Sarah Jane Smith, Luke and his friends Clyde, Rani, and Maria. Mr Smith – an alien computer.

Recommended Reading

In those brief gaps between adventures, you can read up on all sorts of things that will help you with the next adventure. Here's a few suggestions to get you started.

Professor Thrifthead's *Flora and Fauna of the Universe*

Jane's Book of Spacecraft

Time Travel for Dummies

Notes on the Lonely Assassins by Rastan Jovanich

Teach Yourself Everything

Time Lord in Training

I-Spy Book of the Universe

Monster Fighting for Beginners

A Journal of Impossible Things by Verity Newman

This book!

Not Through Choice

Sometimes his companions have to leave the Doctor when they don't want to. Sometimes he lets them go reluctantly. Often there are difficult decisions to be made — the First Doctor locked his granddaughter Susan out of the TARDIS, knowing it would be better for her to stay on Earth to marry Dalek-fighter David Campbell... Occasionally, circumstances conspire to create a situation where they leave even though they don't want to go, and the Doctor doesn't want to lose them.

Katarina
Killed saving the Doctor from having to give in to an escaping convict, who was holding her hostage in a spaceship air lock.

Jamie McCrimmon and Zoe Heriot
The Time Lords wiped their memories of all but their first adventure with the Doctor and sent them home.

Adric
Killed trying to stop a space freighter from crashing into Earth.

Sarah Jane Smith
The Doctor and Sarah Jane had to part company when the Doctor was summoned back to Gallifrey.

Tegan Jovanka
Accidentally left behind at Heathrow Airport by the Doctor. They met again by chance in Amsterdam.

Rose Tyler
Stranded in a parallel world when the gateways between the worlds were closed.

Peri Brown
Reports vary – she may have been killed and her brain removed, or possibly she left willingly to marry the warlord Yrcanos.

Donna Noble
Forced to forget everything about the Doctor to save her life, after she absorbed some of his regenerative energy aboard the TARDIS and became part Time Lord.

Don't Be Deceived

It is said that every individual has a doppelganger – a perfect double who looks exactly like them. In an infinite Universe, it is certain that the same shape and form will recur. For the Doctor, this potential problem is exaggerated. Partly because he has changed his appearance several times, so that means there's more chance of a double. But the Doctor's enemies have also deliberately copied him as part of their dastardly plans.

The First Doctor

As far as we know, he never met the Abbot of Amboise, a 16th century French cleric who was murdered. But the Daleks created a robot double of the Doctor to confuse his companions when they pursued the TARDIS through time and space.

The Second Doctor

Salamander – the self-styled saviour of the world – closely resembled the Doctor, and impersonated him to try to escape in the TARDIS. He was flung off into the Time Vortex when he dematerialised without closing the TARDIS doors.

The Third Doctor

He and Jo Grant met future versions of themselves when the Doctor was trying to mend the TARDIS. The phenomenon was short-lived and their future selves disappeared.

The Fourth Doctor

The dastardly Meglos impersonated the Doctor. But his control over the form broke down, and his true cactus-like appearance broke through. The Kraals also created an android copy of the Doctor – which he then reprogrammed to defeat them.

The Fifth Doctor

Time Lord stellar engineer Omega fashioned his new form on the Doctor's bio-data when he tried to return to our universe from his world of anti-matter. But the form was unstable and broke down.

The Sixth Doctor

As well as an illusion of himself in the Punishment Dome on Varos, the Sixth Doctor saw a version of his actions which he believed had been fabricated as part of the evidence at his trial.

The Seventh Doctor
&
the Eighth Doctor

No reported doubles sighted. So far.

The Ninth Doctor

Not really a double as such, but the Ninth Doctor left a holographic message for Rose in the TARDIS to be played to her in the event of his death. The Tenth Doctor has also left similar emergency messages.

The Tenth Doctor

Another version of the Tenth Doctor grew from the hand that was severed by the Sycorax Leader during a swordfight. Just as the Doctor grew another hand, so later the hand grew another Doctor, who stayed with Rose on a parallel Earth.

The Eleventh Doctor

No doppelgangers sighted so far. But the so-called Dream Lord was a version of this Doctor created from the Doctor's dark side by psychic pollen…

Captain
Jack Harkness

Real Name

Unknown.

Home

Originally from the Boeshane Peninsula.

Spends Time

Former Time Agent. Last seen in charge of Torchwood Three in Cardiff.

Relatives

Father Franklin presumed killed in an alien invasion of their homeworld. His brother, Gray, was kidnapped.

First met the Doctor

Tried to con the Doctor by selling him a Chula warship that crashed in London during the Blitz. In fact it was a Chula medical ship, and Jack helped the Doctor and Rose clear up the problems caused by released nanogenes.

Left the Doctor

Exterminated by the Daleks, Jack
was brought back to life – and
rendered immortal – by Rose, using
the power of the Time Vortex. The
Doctor left him for dead. They later met
in present day Cardiff, where Jack had
been waiting for the Doctor to return to
the Rift. They have remained friends and
sometime colleagues ever since. It is possible
that Jack eventually becomes the Face of Boe
– who the Doctor has met several times, and
who died on New Earth after helping the Doctor
release trapped motorists from the Macra.

Enemies faced

Jack has faced many alien threats
while working with Torchwood,
including the terrible 4-5-6. While
helping the Doctor he has faced the
so-called Empty Child, Slitheen, Daleks,
Futurekind, the Master, the Toclafane
and Davros.

Friends and Allies

Too many to mention, but especially
Martha Jones, Gwen Cooper,
Ianto Jones, and other Torchwood
personnel. Also Rose Tyler,
Donna Noble, and Sarah
Jane Smith.

Words of Wisdom

'Oh, did you have to? "No turning back". That's almost as bad as, "Nothing can possibly go wrong" or "this is going to be the best Christmas Walford's ever had".'
The Tenth Doctor

'Agatha Christie didn't walk around surrounded by murders. Not really. I mean that's like meeting Charles Dickens and he's surrounded by ghosts. At Christmas.'
Donna Noble

You just forget about Christmas and things in the TARDIS. They don't exist. You get sort of... timeless.'
Rose Tyler

'Ladies and gentlemen! I know that man— that Doctor on high. And I know that he has done this deed a thousand times. But not once, no sir, not once— not ever—has he been thanked. But no more, as I say to you on this Christmas morn: Bravo sir! Bravo!'
Jackson Lake

'I shall be taking you to old London town in the country of UK, ruled over by good King Wenceslas. Now human beings worshipped the great god Santa, a creature with fearsome claws, and his wife Mary. And every Christmas Eve the people of UK go to war with the country of Turkey. They then eat the Turkey people for Christmas dinner... like savages.'
Mr Copper

'Doesn't that just sum up Christmas? You go through all those presents and right at the end, tucked away at the bottom, there's always one stupid old satsuma. Who wants a satsuma?'
The Doctor

'Merry Christmas to you. God bless us, every one.'
Charles Dickens

'And so it came to pass on Christmas Day, that the human race did cease to exist.'
Rassilon

Useful Information
How to Write in Code

If you want to send someone a message that no one else can read, then you need to send it in code. There are lots of different ways you can encrypt information, which means put it into code. But obviously you need to use a system that is easy and quick, that isn't too simple for someone else to work out, and that the person you're writing to can understand.

The simplest form of code is a substitution cipher ('cipher' is just another word for code). You just change one letter for another, using a list that both the sender and receiver of the message have a copy of. You can make up your own list, either by randomly changing letters, or using a system like this:

Using the blue code line, the message 'Prisoner Zero has escaped' would be put into code as 'Kirhlmvi Avil szh vhxzkvw'.

A clever way to change the code with every message is to include a word or set of letters that the receiver uses to work out the new code. You can select just random letters, or a code word. Simply use that set of letters for the first letters of the alphabet, then write the rest of the alphabet in order, leaving out the letters you have already used.

So a codeword 'Dalek' would give a code like the green code line.

Using this code, the message 'Prisoner Zero has escaped' would be put into code as 'Kiphglmwi Awil qyh whtykwz'.

If you use a different code word each time, just put that at the start of the message to tell the receiver how to make the new code list – 'Dalek Kiphglmwi Awil qyh whtykwz'.

To	Change	To	Change
Z	A	Z	D
Y	B	Y	A
X	C	X	L
W	D	W	E
V	E	V	K
U	F	U	B
T	G	T	C
S	H	S	F
R	I	R	G
Q	J	Q	H
P	K	P	I
O	L	O	J
N	M	N	M
M	N	M	N
L	O	L	O
K	P	K	P
J	Q	J	Q
I	R	I	R
H	S	H	S
G	T	G	T
F	U	F	U
E	V	E	V
D	W	D	W
C	X	C	X
B	Y	B	Y
A	Z	A	Z

Constellations

The stars in the sky as seen from our planet Earth are grouped into constellations according to where they appear in the sky. Although stars can look very close together, they may be millions of light years apart as we can't tell just by looking which stars are closer and which are much further away.

Originally, the constellations were named after the shapes people thought the stars made if you looked at them together. The signs of the Zodiac are the constellations that lie along the line the sun takes when it crosses the sky.

Of course, other planets have different constellations. The Doctor once claimed he was born under the sign of 'Crossed Computers'.

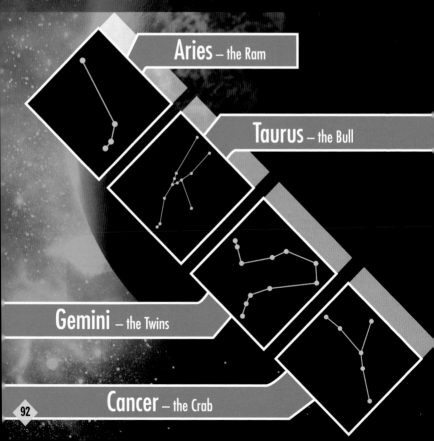

Aries – the Ram

Taurus – the Bull

Gemini – the Twins

Cancer – the Crab

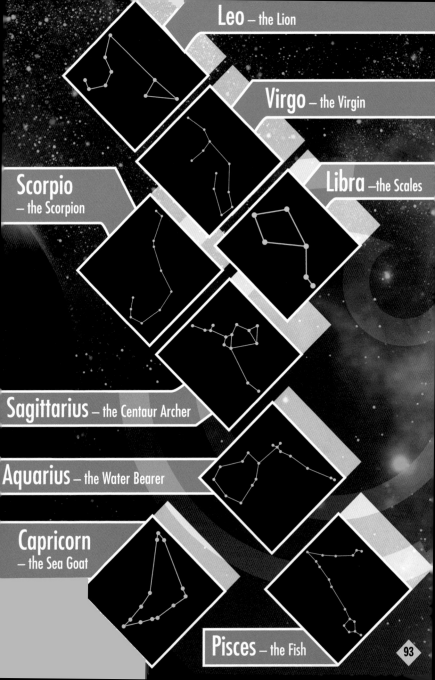

Leo – the Lion

Virgo – the Virgin

Scorpio
– the Scorpion

Libra –the Scales

Sagittarius – the Centaur Archer

Aquarius – the Water Bearer

Capricorn
– the Sea Goat

Pisces – the Fish

Useful
Disguises

The Doctor and his companions often have to go 'undercover' to avoid being recognised or to find out secret information. Over the years, the Doctor has disguised himself as various guards, a robot mummy, a cleaning woman, a milkman — and even pretended to be a Dalek!

Here are a few suggestions of disguises that might be useful.

Police – gives an air of authority. Even the Doctor could be deceived.

Waitress – to infiltrate posh parties or restaurants, etc.

School Dinner Lady – keep an eye on the kids, teachers and other dinner ladies.

Servant Girl – who notices the servants?

Public School Teacher – could be a disguise or a whole new identity.

Posh Party Guest – get to mingle with important and rich people.

Lodger – No disguise necessary.

Mad Science

As well as misguided scientists from his own race, like the beautiful but deadly Rani, the Doctor has encountered many scientists whose work and experiments threatened civilisation. Some believed they were working for the best — Professor Stahlman drilled into the Earth's crust in the hope of discovering a new energy source, not unleashing a primordial terror. Others were just plain mad — Professor Zaroff wanted to destroy Atlantis and flood the world.

But whatever the motivation of the scientists behind it, the Doctor has managed to sort out many experiments and scientific projects. Here are just some of them.

Sisters of Plenitude

The Sisters of Plenitude of New Earth bred human zombies and infected them with every known disease so they could develop and incubate cures within the bodies of the poor 'patients'.

Professor Lazarus

Misguided rather than mad, Lazarus wanted to change what it meant to be human — by rather selfishly making himself younger. While this seemed to work, he later mutated into a huge murderous creature.

Ood Operations

The Doctor put a stop to the company's programme of removing the Oods' hind brains and turning them into docile slaves.

Discovery Drilling

A bona fide scientific project, it discovered more than it expected when intelligent reptiles known as Homo Reptilia (or Silurians) drilled back up to meet the shaft sunk in the Welsh village of Cwmtaff.

John Lumic

Head of Cybus Industries on a parallel Earth, Lumic wanted to upgrade the human race to the next level of evolution. But the development meant replacing human bodies with metal and plastic and removing all emotions – to create the Cybermen.

Davros

On the war-torn planet of Skaro, Kaled scientist Davros realised that his people were mutating because of the biological, chemical, and nuclear weapons used in their war against the Thals. He developed a life-support system designed to sustain the form he knew his people would eventually mutate into. But he hastened that mutation, and changed the nature of the resulting creatures that he installed in the armoured travel machines. Machines that he called Daleks.

The Spotter's Guide
to Spaceships

As you travel through the universe, you will see many spaceships and space stations. Being able to recognise the more common spacecraft can be a huge benefit. If you can distinguish between a Chula Medical Ship and a Dalek Attack Saucer you are more likely to avoid embarrassing circumstances that might otherwise arise.

Here are just some of the spaceships you might encounter on your travels.

Slitheen Scout Ship

Single pilot craft. Can be flown by remote control.

42nd Century Standard Shuttle

This type of shuttle was used on all Sanctuary Bases, as well as by companies like Ood Operations.

Fourth Great & Bountiful Earth Empire Satellite

Standard design as used, for example, for Satellite 5.

Judoon Enforcement Ship

Check you aren't breaking any rules or laws if you see one of these.

Max Capricorn Cruise Liner

Same design as the ill-fated starship *Titanic*.

Sontaran Scout Ship

Carries just one Sontaran. Luckily.

42nd Century Cargo Freighter

Widely used for bulk transport.

Donna Noble

Home

London.

Spends Time

Varies. Mainly temping as a secretary – including at a library, double-glazing company, and H. C. Clements.

Relatives

Donna's father Geoff Noble sadly died. She lives with her mother, Sylvia, and grandfather, Wilf, until she marries Shaun Temple.

First met the Doctor

Was transported into the TARDIS on her wedding day. After helping the Doctor against the Empress of the Racnoss, Donna sought him out again by investigating strange events. She finally caught up with the Doctor at Adipose Industries.

Left the Doctor

The Doctor was forced to remove Donna's memory of him to save her life, after she bonded with his severed hand and subsequently suffered a biological meta-crisis.

Enemies faced

The Empress of the Racnoss, Miss Foster, Pyroviles, Ood Operations, Sontarans, Vespiform, Vashta Nerada, Daleks, Davros, the Master.

Friends and Allies

Martha Jones, Jenny – the Doctor's daughter, Rose Tyler, Captain Jack Harkness, Sarah Jane Smith.

Alias Smith

As well as the occasional disguise, the Doctor often goes under an assumed name. His favourite is John Smith – an alias first given to the Second Doctor by his friend, Jamie McCrimmon, while the Doctor was unconscious aboard the so-called Wheel in Space.

Doctor John Smith

Or sometimes just plain 'John Smith'. This was the name adopted by the Doctor when he was exiled to Earth by the Time Lords. He also used it when he became human and hid at Farringham School.

I. M. Foreman

It's not clear if the Doctor ever actually used this name. But the very first time we met him, the TARDIS was hidden in a junkyard owned by the mysterious I. M. Foreman, and the Doctor's granddaughter called herself Susan Foreman.

Doctor James McCrimmon

Name adopted by the Doctor when he met Queen Victoria in Scotland.

Spartacus

The Doctor used this name in Pompeii. So did Donna.

Doctor Noble

Name by which the Doctor infiltrated a meeting at Ood Operations. He and Donna were keen to stress they were not married, though both represented the (fictitious) Noble Corporation.

Sir Doctor of TARDIS

Not strictly an alias, as this was how the Doctor was knighted by Queen Victoria. It is also how he introduced himself to William Shakespeare.

Escaping from a Locked Cell

Every cell is different, so there is no standard method of escape. In fact, if there was, then the people who put you in the cell would know about it and take measures to prevent you using it.

This simple flowchart may give you some ideas of things you can try, though. Memorise it now — you can't guarantee that you'll get locked up when you just happen to have this book with you. And even if you do, your captors may recognise its immense value and confiscate it.

NO → Wait until someone opens the door.

Have they come to rescue you?

YES

YES

Are they armed?

YES

NO

NO

Do you think you could overpower them?

YES

Bad luck. Looks like you'll have to stay where you are and wait for another opportunity to escape.

START

Is the cell door locked?

YES → Do you have anything to pick the lock?

NO → You're in luck. Just leave.

Do you have anything to pick the lock?

NO → Is there a window, ventillation grille or other possible exit?

YES → Can you or anyone with you manage to pick the lock?

Can you or anyone with you manage to pick the lock?

NO → Can you get out through it?

YES → Pick the lock and leave.

Is there a window, ventillation grille or other possible exit?

NO →

YES → Can you get out through it?

Can you get out through it?

NO →

YES → Is it a viable escape route (not too high or small, not leading into another locked cell...)?

Is it a viable escape route (not too high or small, not leading into another locked cell...)?

YES → Escape this way.

You're in luck, leave with them.

Take them by suprise and escape.

Escape this way.

Pick the lock and leave.

Watch out for guards!

105

Double Trouble

It isn't just the Doctor who has met doppelgängers. On some occasions, his companions too have found themselves facing doubles. Or the Doctor has met people who look just like one of his companions. This may be a chance encounter — when the Doctor first met Martha Jones, he'd already seen her very similar-looking cousin Adeola Oshodi working at Torchwood. Here are some notable companion doppelgängers.

Romana

On the planet Tara, the Doctor met several doubles of his friend Romana. Not only was she identical to Princess Strella, but the despicable Count Grendel created android copies of both Strella and Romana to try to assassinate his rival Prince Reynart – who was himself replaced by the Doctor with an android.

Sarah Jane Smith

The Kraals tried to fool the Doctor with an android copy of Sarah Jane. But the Doctor spotted her, so he wasn't surprised when she drew a gun on him.

Mickey Smith

Rose didn't notice that Mickey had been replaced by an Auton copy – until the Doctor pulled his head off in the restaurant where they were having dinner.

Martha Jones

The Sontarans created a clone of Martha to infiltrate UNIT and stop them opposing the Sontaran plan. The Doctor spotted the clone – who actually thought she was the real Martha.

Centurian Rory

When Rory fell into the crack and 'died' he later turned up again in Roman Britain. Rory had been replaced by an Auton copy – constructed from Amy's memories. The copy was so good that it became almost human and the real Rory returned after the second Big Bang.

Adventure Wear

You never know when adventure may be at hand. So make sure you're dressed for the occasion. Here are some handy fashion tips for would-be adventurers.

Coat

Not always needed, but it's as well to keep a jacket handy. Extra pockets are always useful too — make sure some of them zip up so you don't lose your sonic screwdriver, psychic paper or other important gadgets. Bright colours might be best avoided in case you need to hide.

Trousers or Skirt (girls)

Remember you'll need to be able to run, climb, crawl and leap away from danger – or into it. So a full-length skirt or dress might not be the most practical option, however glamorous it might look.

Gloves

Another useful accessory – especially on cold planets like the Ood-Sphere. Always keep a pair of good, strong, hard-wearing gloves 'handy'!

Footwear

Good sturdy shoes or boots. Trainers are good for running of course, but think about whether you might need to climb.

If it gets incredibly cold, or there are several suns beating down, you might want a hat to keep warm or protect your head. Something fashionable but that can easily be stuffed into a pocket would be useful.

Top

Wear something that won't restrict your movements, especially if there's climbing or fighting to be done!

Trousers (boys)

Loose-fitting as you'll need to be able to run, climb, crawl and leap away from danger – or into it. Lots of big pockets would be useful. You can never have too many pockets.

UNIT Personnel

Many people work for UNIT all across the world. As it's an organisation that prides itself on secrecy, many of them are undercover and you may never realise who they are. Your best friend or your mum or dad could work for UNIT and you might never know.

Personnel you might meet or hear about include:

Brigadier Lethbridge-Stewart
First UK head of UNIT. Now often based in South America

Brigadier Winifred Bambera
Head of UNIT in the UK after Colonel Crichton

Corporal Bell
Administrative assistant to Brigadier Lethbridge-Stewart

Colonel Crichton
Successor to Brigadier Lethbridge-Stewart as UK head of UNIT

Sergeant Benton
UNIT stalwart and friend of the Doctor

The Doctor
UNIT's mysterious scientific advisor. Thought to be a codename as his appearance has changed several times

Major Frost
Killed by the Slitheen at 10 Downing Street

Jo Grant
Assistant to the Doctor

Privates Gray & Harris
Cloned by the Sontarans as part of their stratagem

Sally Jacobs
UNIT technician based at the Tower of London facility

Private Ross Jenkins
Killed by the Sontarans

Doctor Martha Jones
UNIT's medical Officer

Major Kilburn
Actually an alien infiltrator, one of the Bane

General Sanchez
Commander of UNIT in Manhattan. Exterminated by the Daleks

Captain Mike Yates
Left UNIT after the Dinosaur invasion of London

Colonel Mace
In charge of the fight against the Sontarans

Major Blake
Killed by the Sycorax

Doctor Elizabeth Shaw
Scientific Advisor before the Doctor was recruited

Captain Erisa Magambo
Investigated the wormhole that a London bus disappeared into. Also investigated parallel timelines.

Surgeon Lieutenant Harry Sullivan
UNIT's medical officer

Colonel Oduya
Liased with Torchwood

Doctor Malcolm Taylor
Scientific Advisor (some years after the Doctor left UNIT)

Captain Marian Price
Second in command to Colonel Mace

You are the Doctor!

Recognising someone who may have changed their appearance can be a challenge. The Daleks seem able to recognise the Doctor in whatever form he takes, as can K-9. They do this by scanning and recognising his specific metabolic form.

You may not be a Dalek or K-9, but there are some clues you can look for if you think you've met the Doctor and want to be absolutely sure.

Wisdom beyond his years – No matter how young the Doctor looks, he can't disguise his wealth of knowledge and tremendous experience for long.

Sonic Screwdriver – There are not many of these around.

Psychic Paper – If he shows you what seems to be a genuine identity card, but for a rather weird profession or occasion, you might be looking at the Doctor's psychic paper.

Eccentric behaviour – Perhaps the biggest clue of all. There is no one else in the whole universe who is quite like the Doctor.

Body temperature – The Doctor's body temperature can vary – in a self-healing coma he gets very cold. A temperature very different to human normal is a good clue you've met an alien.

Two hearts – You may not be able to whip out your stethoscope to check this, but you never know.

Regeneration – If you see the Doctor regenerate when a human being would die, that is a huge clue.

113

Amy Pond

Home

Leadworth in Gloucestershire, though she's originally from Scotland

Spends Time

Until she met the Doctor again as a grown-up, little Amy spent a lot of her time drawing pictures of him and the TARDIS, and making dolls, hand puppets and Raggedy Doctor toys...

Relatives

Amy lives with her mum and dad, though her memories of them were lost for a while through a crack in time. She is married to Rory Williams.

First met the Doctor

When she was a little girl and the TARDIS crashed into her garden. He told her he'd be back in five minutes, and was gone for 12 years. Then he disappeared for another two years.

Left the Doctor

Not yet known...

Enemies faced so far

Prisoner Zero, the Smilers,
Daleks, Weeping Angels,
Saturnynes, Homo Reptilia,
the Dream Lord, Krafayis,
Cybermen, Autons,
Atraxi...

Friends and Allies

Rory Williams, Liz 10,
Winston Churchill,
River Song,
Vincent Van Gogh...

Star Gazing

All the stars in the night sky might look much the same to you. But there are actually many different types of star. The classification of stars uses a system of letters to group stars into many different types according to their colour and temperature.

Through their lives, stars follow a sequence. At the start of their lives stars are very large, but by the end they are very small.

O – Large blue star. Very bright and hot. 40,000 - 29,000°C

B – Blue-y white star. 28,000 - 9,700°C

A – White star. 9,600 - 7,200°C

F – Yellowy-white star. 7,100 - 5,800°C

G – Yellow star (like our own sun). 5,700 - 4,700°C

K – Orange star. 4,600 - 3,300°C

M – Small red star. Very dim light. 3,200 - 2,100°C

Strange Stars

As they go through their life cycle, stars change considerably. Here are some specific kinds of star you may hear of or encounter.

Dwarf Star

There are several types of dwarf star, distinguished by colour. All are relatively small stars, hence the term. Dwarf Star Alloy is a very dense metal used by Tharil slavers to restrain their time-sensitive captives, as it impedes their ability to slip through time.

Neutron Star

The remains of a star that has collapsed, composed almost entirely of subatomic particles called neutrons. The Tythonians diverted the course of a neutron star so it would destroy the planet Chloris after their ambassador was imprisoned by Lady Adrasta.

Supernova

An exploding star. The light and energy created can outshine an entire galaxy. A supernova may subsequently collapse to become a neutron star or a black hole.

Pulsar

A type of neutron star that emits a beam of electromagnetic radiation as it spins. From Earth, this beam looks like a pulse of energy – just as a lighthouse seems to flash when in fact it emits a rotating beam of light.

Black Hole

An area of space where the gravitational forces are so great that nothing can escape – not even light. The only object that has ever been observed actually orbiting a black hole without being drawn into it was the planet known as Krop Tor – which did fall into the black hole designated K 37 Gem 5 after the Beast was defeated by the Doctor and Rose. The Time Lords detonated stars to create the energy needed for time travel – black holes were a side effect. The first Time Lord stellar engineer – Omega – was lost in the black hole he created...

Last Chance to See . . .

There is so much to see and experience as you travel through space and time that it's impossible to list everything. Just describing the 700 Wonders of the Universe would need a whole series of books like this. But it is worth listing some of the more important of the many endangered species in the Universe, so that you can pay special attention to any of these that you encounter.

The Face of Boe

The last of his kind – whatever that was... Unconfirmed reports suggest that the Face of Boe was actually the incredibly old Captain Jack Harkness. The Face of Boe had children – Boeminas – which he outlived. He eventually died saving the inhabitants of New Earth from the hideous Macra.

Star Whale

There were once millions of Star Whales, living in the depths of space. According to legend they guided the early human space travellers through the asteroid belts and kept them safe. It isn't known how or why they died out, but the last Star Whale carried the population of the UK (excluding Scotland) to safety when they were forced to escape from Earth.

Human Beings

By the time Earth was consumed by the expanding sun, the human race had become so interbred with other species that Lady Cassandra O'Brien

Dot Delta Seventeen claimed to be the last pureblood human. She had undergone so many cosmetic and enhancing operations and procedures that she was no longer recognisable as a human being.

Homo Reptilia

It is not known how many Homo Reptilia actually survive. They went into hibernation millions of years ago to escape the devastation they knew would be wrought by the collision of a small rogue planet with Earth. In fact the small planet never hit Earth, but was captured in its orbit and became the moon. As the catastrophe never occurred, the Homo Reptilia never woke from their sleep.

Daleks

After the Great Time War, the Daleks were all but destroyed. It was thought for a while that the last Dalek survived as an exhibit in a private collection in America. But in fact other Daleks had also survived – including the four Daleks that made up the legendary Cult of Skaro. The last of the Cult of Skaro, Dalek Caan, travelled back to the Time War and rescued Davros – the creator of the Daleks. But even so the race was all but wiped out... Until a new race of Daleks was created from a Progenitor. Now the Daleks are rebuilding their empire, ready once again to make all other life forms extinct.

Weeping Angels

Reports on the Weeping Angels – also known as the Lonely Assassins – vary. At one time it was thought only one Angel survived. But then many more were discovered in an ancient, abandoned Aplan Temple. It is difficult to track their numbers, as when they are observed the Angels are indistinguishable from statues.

Time Lords

The Time Lords too were all but wiped out in the Great Time War. The Master survived by becoming human for a while, but he too is now gone – taking President Rassilon and the last survivors of the High Council with him. The only Time Lord known to have survived is the Doctor – the last of his race.

Blood Suckers

There are many races in the universe that survive by ingesting the blood of others. The chart shows how dangerous some of these creatures are.

10

The Great Vampire

Witch Lords of E-Space

Ogri

Saturnynes

Plasmavore

Haemovores

Deadly

1

Monsters

Galactic
Survival Kit

Going on an adventure through time and space? If you only have five minutes to pack a suitcase before the Doctor returns for you, here are some suggestions of useful things to pack.

Sonic Screwdriver – If you have one

First Aid Kit – Hopefully not needed, but just in case...

FIRST AID

String – Always useful

Mobile Phone – Preferably super-charged for universal calling

Engagement Ring — If applicable

Journal — For keeping notes on your adventures

Teddy — Always a comfort

Toothbrush — Essential. Toothpaste too, if possible

Favourite Clothes — In case the TARDIS wardrobe doesn't have what you fancy

Words of Wisdom

'The Doctor likes travelling with an entourage. Sometimes they're humans, sometimes they're aliens, and sometimes... they're tin dogs.'
Sarah Jane Smith

'Promise me one thing – find someone... Because sometimes, I think you need someone to stop you.'
Donna Noble

'I don't age. I regenerate. But humans decay. You wither and you die. Imagine watching that happen...'
The Tenth Doctor

'Every night, Doctor, when it gets dark and the stars come out, I'll look up. On her behalf. I'll look up at the sky and think of you.'
Wilf Noble

'Well, sometimes I have guests. I mean some friends, travelling alongside. I had... there was recently a friend of mine. Rose, her name was, Rose.'
The Tenth Doctor

Correct Address

You may meet all sorts of important people on your travels. Addressing them correctly when you talk to them is very important for universal diplomatic relations.

POLICE PUBLIC CALL BOX

The Queen — 'Your Majesty' the first time, then you can call her 'Ma'am'.

Royal Princes and Princesses — 'Your Royal Highness' the first time, then you can call them 'Sir' or 'Ma'am'.

Duke or Duchess — 'Your Grace'.

Earl, Viscount, or Baron — 'My Lord'.

Countess, Viscountess, or Baroness — 'My Lady'.

Lord President of the Time Lords — 'My Lord President'.

Draconian Emperor — 'Your Majesty'. If you are yourself a noble of Draconia, you may also use the traditional form of address: 'My life at your command.'

If in doubt
— Be polite!

Mysterious Figures

There are some very strange people and creatures in the universe. The lives and habits of some are well documented. Others remain a mystery. Some of the more mysterious creatures you might encounter include:

The Pantheon of Discord

Little is known of the Trickster – or the creatures that work for him in the Pantheon of Discord – like the Time Beetle that tried to change Donna's life. A shadowy, hooded figure, he revels in the chaos caused by changing history.

The Celestial Toymaker

An incredibly powerful being who has lived for thousands of years, the Toymaker enjoys playing games with his potential victims. If he loses, the price he pays is the destruction of his world, although he always survives and the other player dies. If his opponent loses, they are trapped in his world and become another of his toys.

The Woman

A Time Lord of Rassilon's High Council during the Great Time War. She helped the Doctor indirectly and secretly – by giving advice to Wilf. Her appearance gave the Doctor the strength he needed to defeat Rassilon's plan. But who she is, we don't know. She is obviously someone who cares deeply about the Doctor, someone he respects. Could she even be his mother?

The Dream Lord

An entity composed of the Doctor's own darker instincts, created when the TARDIS Time Rotor was infected with a speck of psychic pollen from the candle meadows of Karrass don Slava. The Dream Lord created a hallucinatory world so real that even the Doctor had trouble distinguishing it from reality.

River Song

A friend and ally of the Doctor – and perhaps much more than that. Amy suspects that River may one day become his wife. The Doctor and River keep meeting at different points in their relative lives, experiencing their adventures out of order. The Doctor knows how River's life will come to an end after facing the Vashta Nerada. But she knows secrets of the Doctor's future too…

Money Money Money

It's all too easy to lose track of what things cost on different planets and at different times. Currencies are not standard across the universe — although the Galactic Credit is gaining ground on the Cosmic Dollar. The chart shows how much of each currency is needed to buy one gram of Jethryk. As the value of money changes over time, the values are given as they will be on the date Eleven / 92 Banana 7.

Value

Cosmic Dollars

Galactic Credits

Pounds Sterling

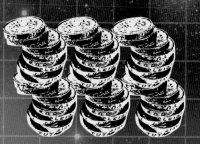

Money

Cathomian Beads

Euros

US Dollars

Danger Signs

It is impossible to predict every type of danger you might face through all of time and space, but to give you some clues — you know you're in trouble when:

You hear any of the following:
- 'Are you my Mummy?'
- 'Burn with me.'
- 'Exterminate.'

- The TARDIS Cloister Bell sounds
- Wheely-bins burp
- The sun explodes
- The dead walk the streets
- A spaceship crashes into Big Ben. Or Buckingham Palace

- You see or hear the words 'Bad Wolf'
  - Scarecrows march
    - A statue moves when you're not looking at it
      - Planets appear in the sky
      - Harold Saxon wins the general election
- A giant wasp tries to sting you
- You have too many shadows
- You hear dead people
- Someone repeats everything you say
- Someone repeats everything you say
- You meet yourself
- The bus you're on goes through a space-time wormhole

- A strange man demands fish fingers and custard
- Daleks seem friendly and offer you a cup of tea
- An invisible enemy is on the prowl
- People don't show up in mirrors
- The Pandorica opens

And above all, you know you're in trouble when you're with the Doctor

Before the Dawn of Time

If you find yourself lucky – or unlucky –
enough to be transported back to prehistoric
times, here are some things to look out for.

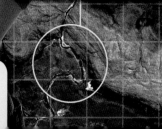

Professor Whitaker – Pioneer of time
travel. Accidentally sent back to the
'golden age' of the dinosaurs

The TARDIS – remember
where you left it and stay
within easy running distance

Volcano Day – Time to leave

The Doctor – Stay close to him, and
keep him out of trouble. If you can

Fissure in Earth's crust –
Keep away. It may lead right
down to the Racnoss nest

Stahlman's Gas – One day it may
be a valuable source of energy. But
there are nasty side-effects

Crashing Space Freighter –
Time to leave! The freighter
fell back through time
and its impact led to the
extinction of the dinosaurs

Tyrannosaurus Rex –
Vicious and carnivorous
dinosaur. Avoid

Other Dinosaurs –
Big and impressive.
Enjoy the view!

Homo Reptilia – Land-based
intelligent reptile people

Homo Reptilia – aquatic and
amphibious intelligent reptiles
known as 'Sea Devils'

Jagaroth spaceship – Keep clear!
The last Jagaroth spaceship
exploded taking off from
prehistoric Earth

Useful Scientific Laws

It is well known that you cannot change the laws of physics – unless you have crossed over the event horizon of a black hole, in which case anything is possible. So you know what you're stuck with, here are a few useful scientific laws.

Heisenberg's Uncertainty Principle

Originally this principle was applied to measuring the speed and position of electrons. Werner Heisenberg showed it was impossible to measure both accurately at the same time. You either know how fast the electron is travelling, or exactly where it is. The term is now often used to suggest that just by observing something, we change the thing being observed and can therefore never be certain that any readings or observations are accurate.

Grimm's Law

This was developed from other people's earlier work by the elder of the Brothers Grimm, famous for their recounting of fairy tales. Grimm's Law explains how sounds change over time as language is developed.

Occam's Razor

Named after William of Occam, a 14th century Franciscan Friar, this principle states that things should not be made any more complicated than they need to be – so the simplest solution to any problem is likely to be the correct one.

The Blinovitch Limitation Effect

Named after Russian scientist Aaron Blinovitch who allegedly developed his theory in a reading room of the British Museum in 1928. He later accidentally put his whole life into reverse and regressed to being a baby. The Blinovitch Limitation Effect is why the Doctor – or any other time traveller – cannot change history. It explains how time lines are inextricably linked together, and warns that if an individual travels back in time and meets him or herself, there will be a colossal release of energy as the timelines merge and short out.

The First Law of Time

The first, and most important, of the Laws of Time developed on Gallifrey during the Old Time states that no one should interfere with the events of history or try to change them. It expressly forbids anyone from meeting a past or future version of him or herself (see also the Blinovitch Limitation Effect). When the Second Doctor was put on trial by the Time Lords, it was in effect for breaking this Law.

Holiday Destinations

With a TARDIS, getting away from it all ought to be easy. But beware – even the most attractive of holiday destinations can be hazardous and conceal hidden dangers. But provided you're alert, there are lots of places in the universe suitable for a nice weekend break.

Midnight

Because of its deadly X-tonic sun, the only safe place on this beautiful planet of glittering diamonds is the Leisure Palace. But excursions to see the stunning Sapphire Waterfall shattering over the Cliffs of Oblivion can be arranged – book early with Crusader Tours.

The Eye of Orion

A noted holiday destination for those wanting a little rest and relaxation. The ancient ruins of a lost civilisation stand above rolling fields and babbling brooks. Art classes available.

Barcelona

Planet where the dogs have no noses, which is something of a talking point. It is not known how the dogs smell. Not to be confused with the Spanish city of the same name.

Woman Wept

The planet got its name from the shape of one of its continents. When viewed from space, it looks like a woman bending over and crying. Some reports suggest that the shape is actually reminiscent of a Weeping Angel... The planet is famous for its thousand mile beaches, which rarely get crowded.

Metebelis Three

Famous blue planet of the Acteon galaxy, noted for its beautiful blue crystals. But if you arrive too early, you may be attacked by huge flying reptiles or primitive natives. If you arrive too late, watch out for the giant spiders that enslaved the human settlers.

Cromer

Caution! That may look like the sandy beaches of Norfolk holiday resort Cromer outside the TARDIS, but you may in fact be over the event horizon of a black hole and looking out on to a world of anti-matter where the physical laws of our universe no longer apply. You can't be too careful.

Rory Williams

Home

Leadworth in Gloucestershire

Spends Time

Rory works as a nurse at the local hospital.

Relatives

Rory is married to Amy Pond.

First met the Doctor

When the Doctor and Amy were trying to find Prisoner Zero. But Rory knew all about the 'Raggedy Doctor' from his childhood games with Amy – where he had to pretend to be the Doctor.

Enemies faced so far

Prisoner Zero, Atraxi, Saturnynes, Homo Reptilia, the Dream Lord, Krafayis, Cybermen, Autons, Daleks...

Left the Doctor

Rory was killed after his encounter with the ancient reptile race known as Silurians. Recreated as an Auton, Rory again met the Doctor and Amy and became human again when his timeline was rewritten and the universe was saved. How and when he later leaves is not yet known...

Friends and Allies

Amy Pond, River Song...

Calling in the Professionals

If the Doctor isn't available, there are several other places you can turn to for help in the event of an alien invasion or other out-of-the-ordinary threat to civilisation as we know it.

Police

Only contact the police if it's a real, non-extraterrestrial emergency. Otherwise they just won't understand and you could be putting them in danger. If you do need the police, officers and cars will respond to all genuine calls.

UNIT

Since it is a secret organisation, contact details for UNIT are rather hard to come by. But if you go to their website, you can log in using the password 'BUFFALO'.

Children of Time

The Doctor has many friends and former companions on Earth, many of whom are in contact with one another. Depending on the situation you could try to contact one or more of the following:

Torchwood

Even more secret than UNIT, for many years no one even knew about Torchwood's existence. Don't try to contact Torchwood. If you need them, they will contact you.

Sir Alistair Gordon Lethbridge-Stewart (formerly of UNIT), retired — may be contacted through the Ministry of Defence.

Captain Jack Harkness — may be contacted through the Ministry of Defence, who will tell you he doesn't exist.

Sarah Jane Smith — lives on Bannerman Road.

Jo Grant — recently taking an interest again in extraordinary phenomena.

Wilf Noble — but do NOT contact his granddaughter Donna Noble.

Mickey Smith & Martha Jones — London area.

Lady Christina de Souza — present whereabouts unknown.

Sally Sparrow — c/o Sparrow and Nightingale Rare Books and DVDs.

Sonic Screwdrivers

The sonic screwdriver has been the Doctor's most trusted and useful gadget for many years. But it has been replaced and redesigned several times.

Original Sonic

The sonic screwdriver was first used by the Second Doctor. Few details are known about this model.

Current Sonic

The sonic screwdriver again burned out when the Eleventh Doctor came up against Prisoner Zero. He has replaced it with an updated model.

River Song's Sonic

At some point in the future, the Doctor gives River Song a sonic screwdriver, which includes a neural relay in which he knows he can save her mind when she dies...

Recent Sonic

The Ninth Doctor relied on his updated sonic screwdriver for a variety of tasks, though it was unable to penetrate a Deadlock Seal. The Tenth Doctor replaced the sonic after it burned out when he destroyed a Slab.

Later Sonics

The Third and Fourth Doctors used the sonic screwdriver for a variety of tasks ranging from undoing bolts to detecting landmines. This sonic was also used by the Fifth Doctor, until it was destroyed by the Terileptils. The Fourth Doctor's companion, Time Lady Romana built herself a more streamlined model. The Eighth Doctor had a similar sonic screwdriver, which he 'inherited' from the Seventh Doctor who presumably created it.

Retail Therapy

There is a saying on the planet Badpun Minimis: 'When you've seen one shopping centre, you've seen a mall.' No matter how carefully you pack for your adventures, there's bound to be something you've forgotten. Knowing the best places to shop as you travel the universe can be a life saver.

Stores

1. **Henriks**
   Large department store. Window displays constantly changing.

2. **Little Shop**
   Several outlets to be found in the Library, Royal Hope Hospital, etc. In case of emergencies, note that the Little Shop will be close to the exit.

3. **Leisure Palace Concession**
   Beauty products and jewellery – diamonds and shattered sapphire a speciality.

4. **Sparrow and Nightingale**
   Antiquarian books and rare DVDs. Easter Eggs available according to season.

5. **Kronk's Burgers**
   Best fast food in the galaxy – just 2 credits 20 for a Kronk Deluxe!

LIFT

FOOD COURT

ENTRANCE
FROM CAR
PARKS

The Truth Behind the Myths

Since our ancestors first started telling each other stories, there have been monsters. Beowulf, one of the first heroes of written fiction battled the monster Grendel — and Grendel's even more frightening mother. The myths of ancient Greece and Rome are filled with creatures and demons. But is there any truth in these myths, or are they just stories?

The Loch Ness Monster

Thought by many to be a surviving dinosaur, there have been reported sightings of the Loch Ness Monster since medieval times. In fact the creature is an armoured cyborg brought to Earth as an embryo by the alien Zygons who rely on its milk to survive. The Doctor thwarted the Zygons' attempt to take over Earth, but the Skarasen survived to live on happily and peacefully in Loch Ness... Sightings of a smaller creature, possibly derived from one of the Morlox of the planet Karfel, have not been confirmed.

Werewolves

The myth of the werewolf goes back centuries. One particularly vivid story centres on the Glen of St Catherine. According to the stories, something fell to Earth, close to St Catherine's Monastery in 1540. Missing children and the sound of howling at the time of the full moon were all blamed on the werewolf that was supposed to have come from that fallen star. It was not until the Doctor and Rose met Queen Victoria at the nearby Torchwood Manor in 1879 that the terrible truth was revealed...

Vampires

The vampire is one of the very oldest and most established creatures of mythology. The stories of vampires range from Dracula to the so-called vampire family of Calvierri. They were active in Venice in 1580 and supposedly opened a school for vampires...

The Minotaur

Half man, half bull, the Minotaur is a creature from ancient Greek mythology, though it is said that a Minotaur existed in ancient Atlantis at the time of King Dalios. The Nimon race bear some similarity to the Minotaur of legend, but they are galactic scavengers that travel from world to world through black holes, plundering their wealth.

Creatures from Fairy Tales

Every planet has its own myths and fairy tales, and Gallifrey is no exception. As well as the tales of the Old Time when even Rassilon was young, there was the story *Blind Fury* which told of the terrible Krafayis – an invisible demon.

London Landmarks

One city in particular seems to have attracted more than its fair share of alien attention. If you find yourself in London with a few minutes to spare between alien invasions, here are a few landmarks you might want to check out.

BT Tower

Formerly the Post Office Tower, the 175m tall concrete and glass tower was opened in 1965 and remained the tallest building in London until 1981. The thirty-fourth floor housed a rotating restaurant, but was for a while home to the insane supercomputer WOTAN that tried to take over London using specially-built War Machines.

Buckingham Palace

The official London home of the Queen, Buckingham Palace was built for the Duke of Buckingham in 1703 (and was then called Buckingham House). It narrowly avoided destruction when the Doctor managed to prevent the starship *Titanic* from crashing into London.

Big Ben

Big Ben is actually the name of the largest bell in what is officially called The Clock Tower of the Palace of Westminster, which was built between 1840-1860 and is home to the Houses of Parliament. If you are flying a spaceship over London, be careful not to hit this tall edifice.

St Paul's Cathedral

There has been a St Paul's Cathedral on the same site on Ludgate Hill, the highest point in London, since 604AD. The present cathedral was designed by Sir Christopher Wren after the previous one was destroyed by the Great Fire of London in 1666. The area around the cathedral has changed over the years, and the famous steps down which the Cybermen marched when they joined with the International Electromatics company to invade Earth have now gone.

The Tower of London

Officially known as Her Majesty's Royal Palace and Fortress, the Tower of London is actually composed of several buildings centred on the White Tower built by William the Conqueror in 1078. It is not known exactly which of the buildings UNIT Headquarters in the UK is beneath.

The London Eye

The largest Ferris wheel in Europe, the London Eye had thirty-two passenger capsules around its edge – representing the thirty-two London boroughs. Each capsule weighs ten tonnes and can carry up to twenty-five passengers. The London Eye can also be used as a circular transmitter.

Southwark Cathedral

Referred to in the Domesday Book of 1086. The current Southwark Cathedral was mainly built between 1220 and 1420. It was here that Professor Lazarus sought refuge after he genetically mutated into a huge monstrous creature.

Westminster Bridge

The bridge of the Thames closest to the Palace of Westminster. If you visit between 2158 – 2164 AD be especially careful, as the bridge is often patrolled by the occupying Dalek forces following their invasion.

Historic Events and Disasters

The chart summarises just some of the events of world history that the Doctor has mentioned he was involved in. It is likely he was present at many others, and of course at less historically significant events in the past.

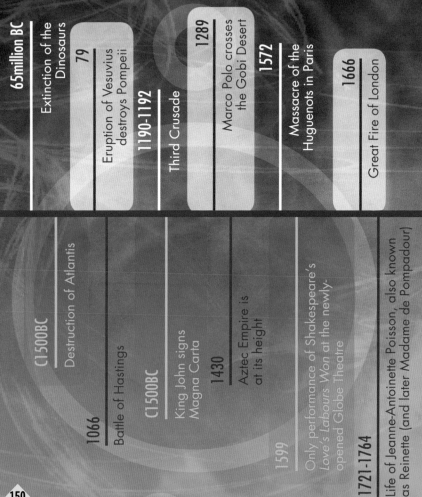

65million BC — Extinction of the Dinosaurs

79 — Eruption of Vesuvius destroys Pompeii

1190-1192 — Third Crusade

1289 — Marco Polo crosses the Gobi Desert

1572 — Massacre of the Huguenots in Paris

1666 — Great Fire of London

C1500BC — Destruction of Atlantis

1066 — Battle of Hastings

C1500BC — King John signs Magna Carta

1430 — Aztec Empire is at its height

1599 — Only performance of Shakespeare's *Love's Labours Won* at the newly-opened Globe Theatre

1721-1764 — Life of Jeanne-Antoinette Poisson, also known as Reinette (and later Madame de Pompadour)

1746

Battle of Culloden effectively ends Scottish rebellion

1869

Charles Dickens visits Cardiff at Christmas

1879

Queen Victoria visits Torchwood Manor and sets up Torchwood Institute

1912

RMS Titanic sets sail on her maiden voyage on 10 April

1926

Novelist Agatha Christie disappears for 11 days

1939-1945

Second World War

1780-1799

French Revolution and ensuing 'Terror'

1872

Mary Celeste found drifting and deserted in the Atlantic

1881

Gunfight at the OK Corral

1914-1918

First World War

1931

Empire State Building completed

1953

Coronation of Queen Elizabeth II

The Colours of the Daleks

Over the millennia, the design of the Daleks has changed as they have discovered new and ever more deadly ways of improving themselves. The Progenitor device activated by the Doctor's testimony created archetypes of each of the four types of Dalek as well as a new Dalek Supreme. Each type is a different colour, as shown here.

Strategist
These Daleks are responsible for planning galactic campaigns as well as battle tactics.

Supreme Dalek
The supreme leader of the Dalek race now that the Emperor no longer exists.

Eternal

No detailed information available –
but this single Dalek has very special
responsibilities. If you discover more,
report it at once to Space Special
Security forces.

Drone

Most Daleks are soldiers
or workers – 'drones'.

Scientist

The Daleks are constantly
developing their technologies
as well as new ways to
exterminate other life forms.

153

Roman Numerals and Other Number Systems

There are many different number systems in use round the universe. As well as the standard Arabic numerals 0 to 9, Roman numbers are also widely used.

The number symbols below are used together to represent the overall number. Numbers that are placed greater to smaller are added together. So, for example, VI means 5+1 and represents 6.

If a small number is placed before a larger one, it is subtracted from that larger number. So, for example, IV means take 1 away from 5 = 4.

I – 1	C – 100
V – 5	D – 500
X – 10	M – 1,000
L – 50	

For multiples of a thousand, a bar can be placed over the number of thousands – so:

$\overline{IV}$ = 4,000

$\overline{M}$ = 1,000,000

Examples

III	1+1+1 = 3
VII	5+1+1 = 7
IX	10-1 = 9
XC	100-10 = 90
CLXXIX	100+50+10+10+(10-1) = 179
MMX	1,000+1,000+10 = 2010

Famous Last Words

The First Doctor
'It's far from being all over. I must get back to the TARDIS immediately. I must go now...I must go at once... Ah yes, thank you. Keep warm.'

The Second Doctor
'What are you doing? No – stop. You're making me giddy. No... You can't do this to me... No... No... No...'

The Third Doctor
'A tear, Sarah Jane? No, don't cry. While there's life, there's...'

The Fourth Doctor
'It's the end. But the moment has been prepared for...'

The Fifth Doctor
'It feels different this time...'

The Sixth Doctor
Last words unknown.

The Seventh Doctor
'Got to stop him...'

The Eighth Doctor
Last words unknown.

The Ninth Doctor
'Rose, before I go,
I just want to tell you,
you were fantastic.
Absolutely fantastic.
And do you know
what? So was I.'

The Tenth Doctor
'I don't want to go...'